Penguin Pandemonium

The Wild Beast

Jeanne Willis

Illustrated by Nathan Reed

For Harriet

First published in Great Britain by HarperCollins *Children's Books* 2013
HarperCollins *Children's Books* is a division of HarperCollins*Publishers* Ltd,
77-85 Fulham Palace Road, Hammersmith, London W6 8JB

Visit us on the web at
www.harpercollins.co.uk

1

Penguin Pandemonium: The Wild Beast
Text copyright © Jeanne Willis 2013
Inside illustrations copyright © Nathan Reed 2013
Cover illustration copyright © Ed Vere 2013
Jeanne Willis asserts the moral right to be identified as the author of this work.

ISBN 978-0-00-749810-9

Printed and bound in England by
Clays Ltd, St Ives plc

Meet the Penguins!

Rory, Eddie & Clive

ROCKHOPPER

Looks: Rockhoppers have spiky yellow and black feathers on their heads that look like long eyebrows.

How big? 45 to 58 cm – about half the size of adult Emperor Penguins.

Favourite food: Shrimps.

Penguin party trick: Rockhopper Penguins love to burst from the water and land on the rocks with a belly flop.

Flipper fact: They hop from rock to rock, keeping both feet together and can jump up to one and a half metres.

Little Blue, Muriel, Hatty & Brenda

Looks: Fairy Penguins have blue feathers on their heads and backs but have white bellies.

How big? 30 to 33 cm – the world's smallest penguin.

Favourite food: Sardines and anchovies.

Penguin party trick: In the wild, Fairy Penguins are nocturnal so they only go on land at night (well past the Rockhoppers' bedtime).

Flipper fact: The world's smallest penguin – they are also known as the Little Penguin, or the Little Blue Penguin.

Paulie, Alaskadabra, Oo-Chi & Ku-Chi (chicks)

Looks: Emperor Penguins have black backs, white tummies and bright splashes of yellow and orange on their front and their ears. The chicks are fluffy and grey and their faces are white, not black.

How big?! Up to one metre tall – the world's tallest and heaviest penguin (over three times as tall as Little Blue!).

Favourite food: Squid.

Penguin party trick: When an egg is laid, the male stands with the egg on his feet to keep it warm until it hatches (this can take up to nine weeks).

Flipper fact: Emperor Penguins can stay under water for nearly twenty minutes!

Waldo, Warren and Wesley

Looks: Chinstrap Penguins get their name from the small black band that runs under their chin.

How big? Up to 68 cm (twice as tall as Fairy Penguins).

Favourite food: Little shrimps called krill.

Penguin party trick: Chinstraps are also known as Stonecracker Penguins because their call is so harsh it sounds like it could break stones.

Flipper fact: Chinstraps are the most common type of penguin – there are about thirteen million of them in the world.

Flighty Almighty

… Ahem, he's a GOOSE!

CHAPTER ONE

Poop, Poopy Do

Saturday at City Zoo was usually the busiest day of the week, but not today. And not last week either. For some strange reason, the crowd that normally gathered to see the penguins had shrunk to almost nothing. It was all very sudden and none of them could understand it, least of all Rory the rockhopper.

Rory had been waiting all morning for people to arrive. He was keen to show off his latest belly-sliding stunt that he'd been practising with his mates, Eddie and Clive, but nobody came. Rory waddled across the snow and gazed up at the webcam suspended above the enclosure. It recorded everything the penguins did and, when they appeared on the internet, people usually came from far and wide to see them. So what had changed?

The way Rory saw it, only two things could have happened: either penguins had gone out of fashion or Penguin Cam had a technical fault. The first reason was unthinkable – everybody loved penguins. It had to be the second reason. It had been a long, hard winter, the frost must have cracked the lens and, as no one could see them in action any more, people might have forgotten that the penguins existed.

Rory decided to investigate, but the camera was high up and his legs were so short he couldn't see, so he jumped up and down as hard as he could, kicking his feet and flapping his flippers to gain some extra height.

"Yoo hoo!" he called. "Is anybody out there? Come and see me! Why don't you *love* me any more?"

"Maybe it's the way you dance," said a voice. "Or are you hopping about because you need the toilet?"

Rory swung round. It was his best friend, Blue, the fairy penguin. He stopped bouncing and pushed back his head feathers to hide his embarrassment.

"That was *not* a toilet dance, Fish Face. I was checking to see if Penguin Cam was broken. If people could see how talented and handsome I am, they'd be here by now."

"Maybe the lens cracked when you looked at it," grinned Blue.

Just then, the two brown bears who lived in the paddock above the penguins butted in. Orson leant over the rails and squinted at the camera.

"There's nothing wrong with it," he said.

"Yes, there is," insisted Ursie, "it's pointing at the penguins instead of the bears. We're far more entertaining – we sing, we dance, we tinkle on the ivories."

Rory's beak fell open.

"You tinkle on the what? Can't you go behind a bush like everyone else?"

The bears looked at him blankly, then, realising he'd misunderstood the phrase, they slapped their furry thighs and guffawed.

"Oooh... I'm laughing so hard, I've tinkled on my ivories!" snorted Ursie, stuffing his paws between his legs.

"Me too!" said Orson. "Just goes to show how little penguins know about entertainment. Fancy not knowing that *tinkling the ivories* is showbiz for playing the piano."

The bears could be very irritating and Rory was beginning to lose his temper.

"You haven't got a piano!" he yelled.

"No, but if we did, it would be a good way to lure the visitors back," said Orson, pretending to play a few imaginary chords. "No one's coming to see us either. Do you know why?"

Rory scratched his head. "Maybe it's

the weather."

"I bet Rory's right," said Blue. "Maybe people can't get to the zoo because of the snow."

Orson shook his head.

"Wrong! There are more visitors than ever, aren't there, Ursie?"

"Record numbers," agreed Ursie, "but they're not coming to see you or us because of You Know Who."

"What's You Know Who, Rory?" whispered Blue.

"You know," he said casually. He had no idea who Ursie was talking about either, but he wasn't going to admit that to the bears – he was hoping that one of them might let it out of the bag without him having to ask. By now, both bears had climbed up their tree to get a better look.

"You should see the queue for the new enclosure below yours," said Orson. "It's enormous!"

"Rory, Orson said it was enormous," hissed Blue. "Maybe it's a new kind of elephant."

Rory shrugged. "I thought he was talking about the queue. Or the enclosure."

Blue spoke to him behind her flipper so the bears couldn't hear. "If it's an enormous enclosure, whatever is in there must be huge, mustn't it, Rory."

Before he could answer, Muriel waddled over with her girly gang of fairy penguins and demanded to know what was going on.

"I hope you're not talking about me behind my back, Bloop," she said. "It's very rude to whisper."

She prodded the smaller of her two friends in the tummy. "Brenda, isn't it rude to whisper?"

"Y…es?" whispered Brenda.

Muriel was very bossy and Brenda found it much easier to agree with everything she said, even if she didn't.

"Actually, Muriel, we've got better things to talk about than you," said Blue.

Muriel preened herself and did a little shimmy.

"Really? I don't think so. What could

possibly be better than me?"

Blue pointed down below. "There's a new animal in there. We're not sure what it is, but we think it's very large."

Muriel put both flippers round the tubbier member of her gang and measured her chubby waistline. "What? Larger than Hatty?"

"I'm big-boned," wailed Hatty.

"*Much* larger than Hatty," said Blue. "And let's hope it's not as mean as you are."

Muriel twisted her beak into a sneer and was trying to think of a witty reply when Orson and Ursie burst into song.

"What is the terrible beast in the zoo?
Nobody knows and we haven't a clue.
A hippophant, maybe? A rhinoceroo?
What is it? Why is it? How is it? Who?
Maybe it's an Elephong covered in hairs,
A great woolly mammoth – like anyone
cares.
Whatever it is that lives under the stairs,
It can't be as fabulous as the brown bears!"

Whatever it was, the crowd below had grown bigger. Even the singing bears couldn't draw their attention away from the mysterious new exhibit. Muriel went over to the viewing grille in the wall of the penguin enclosure, poked her beak through and looked down on to the rows of heads below.

"What's the big attraction?" she screeched. "What are you looking at? You should be looking at *me*!"

Not one person turned round and if there was one thing Muriel hated, it was being ignored.

"I'm not standing for this, are we, Hatty and Brenda!" she raged, grabbing them both by the flippers. "Come along, we're going to teach those visitors to look up to the penguins."

"How?" said Hatty. "Are we going to sing a song?"

"Are we going to do a cute group hug in front of them?" wondered Brenda.

Muriel put her flipper down her throat and gagged.

"No, I'm sick of cute, they're sick of cute. We're going to have to play dirty… Poop, poop!"

She marched them over to the viewing grille, sat down and pushed her tail through the hole above the crowd.

"Hatty," frowned Brenda, "did Muriel mean it when she said *poop*?"

"She must have done. She said it

twice," said Hatty.

Muriel squeezed her eyes shut.

"Stop twittering and poop! Aim for their hats, girls… One, two, three and FIRE!"

Blue and Rory stared in disbelief as Muriel and her friends lifted their tails and squirted droppings all over the visitors. Some of them thought it had started to rain, but when they smelt what had landed on them, they realised it was nothing to do with the weather and everything to do with the row of little birds sitting above them.

"*Made you look, made you stare, penguin poop is in your hair!*" cackled Muriel, dancing up and down triumphantly. Even the brown bears were shocked.

"Imagine if *we'd* done that instead of going in the woods," grunted Orson.

"Terrible behaviour," said Ursie. "I wish we'd thought of it."

Muriel didn't care what anyone thought. She was so pleased with herself, she didn't notice that the penguin keeper had arrived and was being set upon by angry visitors, demanding that he paid their dry-cleaning bills. Rory watched the scene and put his head in his flippers.

"Muriel, how could you stoop so low?"

"Easy! I just bent my knees," she sniggered. "Hatty, Brenda, did you hear my joke? Rory said, 'How did you stoop so low?' And I said, 'I just bent my knees...' Now *laugh*!"

"Ha ha," said Hatty flatly, deeply ashamed of what she'd just done.

"Hee hee," said Brenda, who was even more embarrassed.

But when feeding time came, Muriel finally understood that what she'd done wasn't funny in the slightest. Thinking that the fairy penguins must have terrible upset stomachs after the pooping incident, the keeper was afraid that the other penguins might catch the same bug and dosed their supper with medicine. It tasted so awful, even Rory's permanently hungry friends, Eddie and Clive, were struggling to force it down.

"Does this mackerel taste fishy to you, Clive?" said Eddie.

"Don't be squidiculous," said Clive. "Of course it tastes fishy, it's fish— *Eughh…* No, it's not, it's foul!"

Big Paulie, the boss of them all, took one peck and choked so hard, Rory had to slap him on the back.

"This fish has been tampered with!" spluttered the mighty emperor penguin.

"I think it's been medicated," said Blue, gargling with snow to try and get rid of the taste. Paulie sniffed the fish and screwed up his beak.

"Medicated? Nobody's ill. What's going on?"

None of the penguins said a word, but they all found themselves staring at Muriel, who was trying to hide behind

Hatty and Brenda.

"What?" said Muriel. "Why is everyone looking at me?"

Big Paulie flapped his fish in her face.

"Is the reason I'm having to swallow this, something to do with you?"

"It was Hatty and Brenda!" blurted Muriel. "Wasn't it, Brenda and Hatty?"

Blue was about to leap to their defence when the brown bears stuck their noses in and told Paulie the whole story. When he heard about the pooping plot, his eyebrow feathers shot over the back of his head and, throwing his flippers up in the air, he confronted the ringleader.

"You did this to our visitors? You pooped on the people who pay for our pilchards?"

Muriel shuffled her feet. "I was only trying to get them to come and see *us* instead of the new animal."

"*Animal shmanimal!*" snapped Paulie. "I'm not interested. We are a polite and dignified species and, thanks to you, our reputation has just gone down the toilet. I'm ashamed to be called a penguin."

"It was just a joke," muttered Muriel, nudging Brenda sharply in the ribs.

"Ha ha," said Brenda nervously.

"*Do I look like I'm laughing?*" screeched Paulie. "I was going to give you all a wonderful surprise, but, thanks to Muriel, you can forget it!"

All the penguins took a step backwards

as he stomped over to his palace without a second glance.

"I wonder what the surprise was?" sighed Blue.

"We'll never know now, will we?" said Rory.

Muriel stopped looking at her feet and turned on him.

"Oh my cod! Why is everyone blaming *me*? It's not my fault – is it, Hatty and Brenda?"

But Hatty and Brenda were so upset about not having a surprise, they pretended to be deaf.

"No one is going to come and visit us now. Not after what you did," said Blue.

Seeing that no one was on her side – not even her best friends – Muriel had no option but to try and win everybody back, including the visitors.

"I'll make it up to you," she said. "I have a brilliant plan. You're going to *love* me for it."

28

"I wouldn't go that far," said Rory. "But let's hear it, anyway."

Muriel folded her flippers and took a deep breath.

"All right, I'll tell you... in the morning," she said. "Meet me at Waldo's hutch at dawn."

CHAPTER TWO

Doodahs and Minkies

Morning came, but there was still no sign of Muriel and her "brilliant plan" to bring the visitors back. Blue and Rory had been standing outside Waldo's hutch in the snow since sunrise.

"It's the weekend. Maybe she's having

a lie-in," shivered Blue.

"She's lying, all right," said Rory, stamping his frozen flippers. "Muriel hasn't got a plan; she's all beak. She's not coming."

They were just about to leave when Waldo flung his door open.

"What are you doing out there, darlings?" squealed the chinstrap penguin. "You'll catch your death! We might originate from the Antarctic, but this weather is enough to freeze the bits off an Inuit... Come in!"

He ushered them into the warmth of his hutch. It was too warm, if anything, because, among the numerous items of lost property left behind at City Zoo over the

years, there was a disposable barbecue, which Waldo had just lit with a box of matches stolen by the elephant from its keeper's pocket.

There was an unwritten rule among
the animals that any items of interest
they found should be passed to Waldo,
who used them to create collages and

sculptures with his fellow artists, Warren and Wesley. They were already in the hutch, sitting at the table in front of a box of bits-and-pieces, and were making something. While it came as no surprise to see the Arty Party Penguins there, Rory and Blue hadn't expected to see the peculiar-looking creature perched on Warren's knee. It was roughly the size of a fairy penguin, but had pink curly fur, a pair of antennae and a brightly coloured tail tied along its length with red ribbons like a fancy kite.

"Good morrow," said Warren, looking up briefly from his handiwork.

"Hi," said Rory, "What are you making?"

"A terrible mistake," Warren replied,

shifting uncomfortably under the weight of whoever it was on his lap.

Whoever it was gave his false moustache a sharp tug. "Oh my cod! It is *not* a mistake, Warren. It's a brilliant concept!" it screeched.

Blue did a double take.

"Muriel, is that... you?" The voice sounded familiar, but it was hard to be certain because she was wearing a sequinned mask.

"No, it's not me, Bloop," said Muriel. "The visitors don't want to see the likes of me and you, do they? They want to see something far more chichi than penguins, which is why I am now a parrot of Paradise."

She hopped off Warren's lap, did a little twirl and her tail fell off.

"Don't you dare laugh, Rory!" she snapped. "It's your turn next."

Rory frowned. "What? Is this your amazing plan?"

"Yes! We are all going to disguise ourselves as rare exotic species," she insisted, rooting around in Wesley's box. She pulled out an old shuttlecock and wedged it on his head. "You can be a dodo."

"I don't want to be a dodo!" said Rory, pulling it off with a loud *plop*. "This is madness."

Just at that moment, there was a knock at the door.

"That will be the others," said Muriel enthusiastically as Warren glued her tail back on. "I told them to meet me here for a costume fitting. Don't look at me like that, Bloop. We're all in this together. You can be a purple-crested booby."

Hatty and Brenda were the first to arrive.

"Where's Muriel?" said Hatty, looking round irritably.

"I don't know," tutted Brenda. "Trust her to make us get up early and not be here on time."

"That is soooo like Muriel," said Hatty. "She is *such* a pain in the tail feathers."

Blue was miming frantically to the fairy penguins to shush, but they thought she was waving.

"Hello, Blue," waved Hatty. "You haven't seen Bossybeak, have you?"

Blue cringed. "Who? I don't know who you're talking about."

Brenda looked confused.

"You must do. *You* gave Muriel that nickname in the first place. 'Muriel is such a bossybeak,' you said, and we all laughed."

It was an awkward moment. Even the Arty Party Penguins were shrivelling in their seats.

The parrot of Paradise whipped round, put its flippers on its hips and snorted. "Well, *I* think that Muriel is wonderful."

"You wouldn't say that if you knew her like we do," said Hatty.

"She's a nightmare," agreed Brenda.

Muriel lifted her mask menacingly and glared at them. Brenda and Hatty gulped, clapped their flippers over their eyes and the room fell uncomfortably silent.

"We were talking about a *different* Muriel," said Brenda finally, "weren't we, Hatty?"

"Yes," blurted Hatty, "weren't we, Blue?"

"Were we? We were!" said Blue hastily. "We were talking about Muriel the… erm… the emu. You must have heard the bears talking about her. She's so bossy, isn't she, Rory?"

"Muriel the erm?" said Rory. "Yep… she's a… real bossybeak. And always late for things, according to Orson."

Muriel narrowed her eyes, but decided to carry on regardless.

"So! What do you think about my marvellous plan to dress everyone up to get the visitors back?" she asked the hutch in general. By now, Alaskadabra, the old emperor penguin, had arrived, along with Eddie, Clive and Oo-chi and Ku-chi, the chicks.

"I think it's a great idea," lied Blue, hoping to get back into Muriel's good books.

"It's not great, Bloop, it's the work of a genius," boasted Muriel. "Hatty and Brenda, aren't I a genius?"

The two fairy penguins nodded so hard that Blue was worried their heads might come off.

"Genius. Love you, Muriel!" said Brenda.

"Love you more!" said Hatty. "Hate the emu!"

One of the chicks looked at Hatty sideways.

"What emu? There ith no emu!" insisted Oo-chi, poking her brother in the ribs. "Ku-chi, there ith no emu at Thitty Thoo, ith there?"

Ku-chi thought hard. "No. There'th jutht a thmelly old othstrich."

Anxious to avoid a scene, Waldo whisked the chicks out of Muriel's earshot and, encouraging them to form an orderly queue with the other penguins, he whipped out his tape measure. As he measured everyone up, Wesley and Warren rummaged through the box of hats, gloves and trimmings, trying to find stuff to make into the crazy costumes that Muriel had designed. Apart from Alaskadabra who liked to dress up at the drop of a hat – and he often dropped his hat – the rest of the birds were embarrassed.

"But I don't want to be a *beamingo*!' said Eddie as Wesley stitched him into a brown fur muff and snapped a party tooter on to his beak. "I don't even know what one is!"

"It's a cross between a beaver and a flamingo," said Muriel. "People will pay good money to come and see that. Now keep still, shut up and put these leather mitts on your feet."

Waldo walked among the disgruntled penguins, adjusting elaborate crests made from hat bobbles, pinning on fabric wings and fashioning magnificent horns out of walking-stick handles.

"Me ith a pigmy rhinotheroth!" giggled Oo-chi. "What ith you, Ku-chi?"

Ku-chi scratched his fluffy head and gazed at his sister as if she was stupid. "Me ith a *penguin*, thilly."

Oo-chi wiggled her tail and pouted. "No, you ithn't, ith he, Mithster Waldo? Not any more. You ith a... fluffy hamthster."

"Yes, he's a fluffy hamster," agreed Waldo, stroking the mohair on the cardigan sleeve he had pulled over Ku-chi's head. Ku-chi, however, had other ideas and threw a tantrum.

"I doethn't want to be a thoppy hamthster. I wanth to be an *emu*!" he cheeped.

Waldo took no notice and sewed him into the costume.

"You'll be a hamster and like it, darling," he said. "We've got limited props. It's just a bit of fun."

Just then, Rory caught sight of himself in a wing mirror that had fallen off a zoo truck and was now attached to the wall of Waldo's hutch.

"I look a right sprat!" he exclaimed.

"No change there, then," smirked Muriel, preening her new tail. "Is everybody dressed? Good, because we need to practise our growls and squeaks."

The penguins looked at each other in bewilderment. Even Alaskadabra – disguised as a glider monkey – looked a bit worried.

"Oh dear," he said, "I didn't realise it was a *speaking* part."

Muriel groaned. "It's called *method acting*, love. We're no longer penguins, so we mustn't *sound* like penguins."

Alaskadabra put his head on one side. It was hard to see or hear out of the balaclava that had been pulled over his head. Warren had made a pair of woolly ears by wrapping two elastic bands very tightly round the knitted fabric, which had made the eyeholes shift – the only way Alaskadabra could see out now was through the gaps in the stitches.

"That's all well and good, dear," he said, "but I don't know what a glider monkey sounds like."

"*Ooh, oooh, ah ahhh!*" shrieked Eddie.

"See, even Eddie can do it," said Muriel witheringly.

"I didn't mean to," said Eddie. "Warren just stuck a pin in my bottom."

Warren swore it was an accident and, as Muriel wouldn't take no for an answer, the penguins went into pairs and practised their new bellows, grunts and squeaks. They were encouraged by Waldo, who knew a thing or two about the theatre, but sadly, very little about animal noises. As the din reached a crescendo, there was a sharp rap on the hutch door, but nobody heard it. Suddenly, it flew open.

"What the frozen fillet are you all

playing at!" yelled Big Paulie.

The cackles, moos and roars petered out and the strange menagerie of exotic beasts stared at their assorted feet, unable to look the boss in the eye.

"I could hear you from my palace!" he complained. He held his flippers behind his back and marched up and down, looking at the thinly disguised penguins with a pained expression on his face.

"What *do* you look like?" he wailed.

"Well, sir, I look like a glider monkey. At least I'm trying to," said Alaskadabra.

Paulie put his head in his flippers. "Well, stop trying. It is not a good look. You are an emperor penguin, the noblest of birds. Why would you dress yourself up as a primate? *Why?*"

He turned round and gazed at Blue in disbelief. "And what are you meant to be?"

"A booby," she muttered.

Paulie shook his beak. "Well, somebody's made a booby."

Unfortunately, Warren mistook this for a compliment, leapt up and shook Paulie by the flipper. At last his skills in the wardrobe department seemed to have been recognised.

"Thank you! I made the booby along with most of the costumes. I'm rather handy with a needle."

"It's for a good cause," added Waldo.

"I don't care if it's to save the polar ice cap – take that silly hat off, Rory. You're a disgrace to penguin-kind."

Rory hung his head. "I'm meant to be a dodo."

"No wonder they're extinct," said Paulie. "They must have died of shame."

Seeing that her plan had backfired, Muriel whipped off her false tail and pointed at Blue.

"Yeah, Rory. Who's silly idea was this, anyhoo?"

His beak fell open. "Yours, Muriel!"

She looked bemused. "It was Bloop who said it was a good idea, wasn't it, Hatty and Brenda? Don't deny it." And under her breath she hissed at them, "I still haven't forgiven you for *Muriel the erm*. I wasn't hatched yesterday."

But Hatty and Brenda were very fond of Blue. She always defended them when Muriel got particularly bossy... but which was worse: to drop Blue in it or fall out with Muriel? No contest.

"Blue thought it was a good idea," said Hatty.

"A great one," said Brenda.

Rory hated to see the girls ganging up on his best friend and was just about to stick up for Blue when Paulie stamped his foot.

"Ladies, do *not* point the flipper of blame!" he cried. "That's not how penguins behave. What kind of creatures are you, making Blue a scapegoat?"

"She's not a goat, she's a booby," said Eddie. "I'm a beamingo and Clive's a... What are you, Clive?"

"A feather boa constrictor," muttered Clive, trying not to sneeze as the downy stole he was wrapped in tickled his beak.

Paulie looked as if he was about to explode.

"We are not doodahs or minkeys or mingos!" he bellowed. "Let me spell it out for you – we are "P-E-N-G-W-I-N-S.""

"That's not how you spell penguins," whispered Brenda.

"He's the boss, he can spell it how he likes," replied Hatty.

Oblivious to their backchat, Paulie continued his rant. "Penguins are intelligent birds! Why pretend to be something you're not?"

Nobody answered. It seemed like a silly idea now, but they'd all gone along with it.

"Tell him, Rory," said Muriel, pushing him forward, "or I'll have words with Bossybeak."

Rory took a deep breath and tried his best to explain.

"Paulie, it's like this. Muriel thought – and we all agreed... sort of – that if we looked more... er... interesting, the visitors might come back and see us, instead of the new exhibit."

Paulie listened and nodded. He could be frightening, but he was a wise old bird with a big heart. He'd lived in the penguin enclosure longer than any of them. He'd watched the fairy penguins, rockhoppers and chinstraps grow from fluffy chicks to the fine penguins they were today and, as a mighty emperor, he felt it was his duty to care for them all; he always had done, for as long as they could remember.

"Rory, Rory," he clucked, "I don't know what kind of beast is drawing in the crowds and I don't want to know. It could be a unicorn for all I care. Nothing stays a novelty forever. New animals soon become old hat, but penguins have stood the test of time. Penguins will always be popular. The visitors will be back."

"But *when?*" said Muriel. "I want them here now! I did my feathers specially."

Paulie wagged his flipper at her. "Patience! The zoo is not all about us, Muriel. Now have some pride and go and be penguins."

Paulie turned and waddled out of the hutch. As he disappeared across the snow, the penguins slipped out of their costumes, pulled off their false noses, udders and horns and put them back in the Arty Party prop box.

"Well, I thought we all looked fab," sulked Warren.

"Hey ho," said Wesley. "Paulie might know a lot of things, but he knows *nada* about fashion."

Muriel wasn't happy either. "I don't care what Paulie says, this zoo *is* all about me! Am I the only one who wants to know who's attracting the attention away from us?"

Rory had to admit he was curious.

"If you're half the penguin you think you are, you'd go and find out," insisted Muriel.

Rory, who was very much a whole penguin, accepted the challenge.

"I'll do it tonight!" he said. "Who's coming with me?"

CHAPTER THREE

The Abominable Snowbeast

As the moon rose over City Zoo, a cluster of assorted penguins tiptoed silently across the snow and gathered by the wall of their enclosure.

"Rory, where's Muriel?" said Eddie, clattering with his snowboard.

Rory shushed him urgently. "Quiet! You'll wake Orson and Ursie. Muriel said she had to see a bear about an emu, but really she just chickened out."

"PARDON? CLIVE, WHY IS RORY WHISPERING?" shouted Eddie.

Rory sighed. He'd taken on the role of leader of the expedition to spy on the new exhibit, but if they got caught, it would be his neck on the line. Now Ursie had woken up. Ursie would tell Orson and, before they got back, the whole zoo would know what they'd been up to and Big Paulie would be furious. He still hadn't quite forgiven them for escaping over the wall the last time, when Oo-Chi and Ku-chi went missing.

"Oh, flippers. We've been spotted," said Blue.

Rory glanced up and saw the shadowy figures of two portly bears looking down in their direction.

"Going somewhere?" called Ursie.

"No. We're just... having a midnight feast under the stars," lied Rory.

Eddie's eyes lit up. "Are we, Rory? Cool! Clive, we're having a feast. That will be much more fun than going to find out what that weird new animal is... Where's the food? Is it squid? Is it crab? Is it oysters?"

Orson sniffed the air. "Somebody's lying. I smell porky pies."

"Ooh... are there pies?" whooped Eddie.

It was all too easy to fool Eddie, but

there was no fooling the bears.

"We know where you're going," said Ursie. "You're going to see the abominable snowbeast."

"You'll never come back alive," added Orson. "It eats penguins for breakfast."

Clive and Eddie exchanged nervous glances, but Rory wasn't fazed. The bears were famous for getting their facts wrong, mainly because the wild squirrels kept feeding them false information just for a laugh.

"Don't listen to the bears," he said, trying to reassure everybody. "They're just trying to scare us. There is no such thing as an abominable snowbeast."

"That's what they said about the duck-billed platypus!" hollered Orson. "And as we speak, he's living with his wife and kids by the beavers."

Rory shrugged. "I'm not scared. Whatever it is, it can't eat us if we just look through the window. Come on, guys, let's form a penguin pyramid, like we did last time, and climb over that wall. Eddie, go on the bottom with Clive."

To his surprise, Eddie promptly sat down on the ice.

"Not on *your* bottom, the bottom of the pyramid," explained Blue, helping him up.

As Blue climbed on to Clive and Eddie's shoulders, the bears were still watching.

"Don't tell Big Paulie where we've gone, will you?" said Rory.

"Hmm," said Orson, "what's it worth?"

Rory couldn't think of anything to bribe the bears with. He could have promised to give them his lunch for a week, but they weren't that keen on the squid and sprats that made up the largest part of the penguins' diet.

"We're very partial to salmon," said Ursie. "Big Paulie gets salmon on a Sunday, you know."

"Promise us some salmon and we'll keep our muzzles shut," said Orson.

"We promise. Go back to sleep," said Blue as Rory stood on her shoulders and hauled himself up on to the wall. He pulled a face. "We *promise?* Are you crazy, Blue? If I pinch Paulie's salmon, he'll throw me to the sharks."

There was no telling what Paulie might do when he was angry. He'd done some scary things when he lived in the wild – according to the seagulls – but, as Blue reminded him, they were worse gossips than the squirrels.

"All the emperors get salmon," she whispered. "Alaskadabra will let us have his if we explain."

By now, all the penguins on the mission were sitting on the wall, ready to go over the top. It was a lot higher than they remembered and they might have thought twice about throwing themselves off in the summer, but there was a thick snowdrift below, so they wouldn't hurt themselves.

"One, two three... JUMP!" said Rory.

Apart from Eddie, who couldn't count, they all landed perfectly.

"Just as well I fell on my head and nothing important," said Eddie as Clive pulled him up and dusted him down. "Lead on, Rory, I'm right behind you."

"No, you're in front of me, Eddie," said Rory. "Turn round, we're going *that* way."

The penguins followed silently as Rory made his way down the steep steps to the enclosure below. At one time, it had housed mountain goats and a herd of moose, but they'd been moved to another part of the zoo; it had been empty for months. Building work had taken place because, according to the squirrels, the pool had sprung a leak after a moose put his hoof in it, but none of the penguins were prepared for what they saw.

"Wow," said Rory. "It's got a huge cave with a waterfall and everything!"

"And it's got a much deeper pool than ours," noted Blue. "It must be a very huge animal."

"Like an abdominal snowbeef?" wondered Eddie.

Rory scanned the shadows. He was nervous in case something leapt out and roared, but to his great relief, there was no sign of the creature. However, to one side of the cave, there was a small, dimly lit window made of thick glass – too thick, hopefully, to smash with a massive paw.

"Go on then, Rory," said Blue.

As he crept over, his heart was in his beak. What if the Terrible Mysterious Thing shouted "BOO!", broke the pane and grabbed him? He was scared of losing his cool in front of Eddie and Clive, but now that he was up close, he realised that while the window was the perfect height for a child to see in, it was too high for a rockhopper, even if it jumped.

"Shame," said Rory after the third jump. "Ah well, at least I tried."

"Try harder. We'll give you a leg-up," said Clive.

There was no getting out of it. Rory put his foot in Clive and Eddie's flippers and pulled himself on to the window ledge.

"What can you see?" asked Eddie.

"Nothing," said Rory. "Too dark."

"It might help if you didn't have your eyes shut," Blue pointed out.

He opened them and gasped.

"What is it?" said Blue.

"It's a... Crikey!"

Eddie scratched his head and Rory almost lost his footing.

"What's a *crikey*, Clive?" he asked. "Is it

like a camel only spiky?"

"It's just an expression," explained Clive patiently. "What can you see, Rory?"

Rory's legs were shaking. "It's big and white and furry. It's got a great big head and a long, blobby nose... Oh, hang on, that might be its tail... and it's asleep," he whispered.

"Get down and let me see," insisted Blue.

Rory bent over and she stood on his back, peered through the window and squeaked.

"It's... it's an *abominable snowbeast*, isn't it!"

"It might be," said Rory, "but don't tell Orson and Ursie. They'll be unbearable if they're right."

Blue panicked and nearly fell backwards.

"Arghh… it's waking up!"

"Everybody run!" said Rory.

It wasn't easy to run in the snow and, as the penguins scrabbled about and tripped over each other trying to make their way up the slippery steps to their enclosure, there was a worse sight to come. Having formed a wobbly pyramid and tumbled back over the wall, they were confronted by an angry-looking Paulie and some very worried fairy penguins.

Paulie pointed to the zoo clock and tapped his foot. "What time do you call this? Yet again, you've gone over the wall deliberately and on purpose!"

Rory caught his breath and was about to explain himself when Muriel opened her beak.

"Oh my cod, Rory," she said. "You are *such* a bad penguin. I told you not to go, but you wouldn't listen, would he, Hatty?"

"I wasn't listening," said Hatty.

"We thought you'd been eaten!" wailed Brenda. "You had a little cry, didn't you, Muriel?"

Muriel was about to throttle Brenda when the Arty Party Penguins arrived with a flip chart and pens.

"The bears told us where you'd gone," said Waldo. "We were so worried; was it a frightful beast?"

Rory nodded furiously. "Great… big… furry… huge… horrible…" he panted.

"Massive fangs and… and… and claws!" puffed Blue.

Wesley and Warren pulled the lids off their pens and, listening to the vivid description, they began to scribble down the features of the terrifying animal.

"Enormous horns… hundreds of toes… wings like an elephant!" added Eddie, who hadn't even seen it.

Waldo looked at him sideways. "Hmm… I don't suppose anyone thought to bring an eraser."

But the Arty Party Penguins were unstoppable.

"Wings, Wesley! Draw the wings, love,"

said Warren. "Oh, that's so realistic, it's better than a photograph!"

Rory put his head on one side and squinted at the portrait. It didn't look anything like the creature he'd seen, but was that because he'd described it badly or because Wesley and Warren couldn't draw? He didn't like to say, so he kept quiet. The bears, however, had plenty to say and would not shut up.

"It's an abominable snowbeast, plain as the beak on your face," said Orson.

"Told you so," added Ursie. "I'm surprised the zoo has permission to keep it."

"Me too," insisted Orson. "That monster goes way beyond the Dangerous Animals Act. I shan't sleep a wink in my bed."

"You can share mine," said Ursie, "as long as you don't snore."

As far as Rory could see, the only good thing to come out of all this was that he wouldn't have to give the bears any salmon – not now they'd grassed him up to Paulie. He waited to see what his punishment would be. It was bound to be something awful, like babysitting the chicks or changing the pebbles in the boss's toilet.

"I'm sorry, Paulie," he said, "but I had to find out for all our sakes."

Paulie shook his head solemnly. "Rory, sometimes rules are made to be broken, but this was not one of those times! You put yourself and your friends in grave danger and for what? We can't make the monster go away. All we can do is keep out of *its* way."

He waddled over to the wall and stood there as if he was on guard.

"Go to bed," he ordered, "and don't even *think* about sneaking back over this wall to visit that beast! Do I have your promise?"

"Yep, you do!" said Muriel. "What kind of idiots would do a crazy thing like that?"

Rory and Blue looked at each other knowingly and, as the other penguins hurried back to their nests, they hung back, went into a huddle and began to hatch a plan.

CHAPTER FOUR

Frosty

After a restless bedtime ruined by terrible dreams about the abominable snowbeast, Blue went round to see Rory. He'd had no sleep either and looked very bleary-eyed.

"Did you have nightmares too?" she asked.

Rory nodded. "Yeah, about Muriel."

Blue looked at him sideways. "Not about the snowbeast?"

"That was in it too," he admitted. "It was almost as scary as her. You know what we agreed last night about going back over the wall to find out if the beast is as abominable as it looks...?"

"I'm still up for it," said Blue, "if you are."

"Good," said Rory. "It's not like we promised Paulie we wouldn't – that was Muriel and she's not the boss of us."

Muriel, however, liked to think she was – and she could get Hatty and Brenda to do whatever she asked – but although Blue was the smallest fairy penguin in the pool, she was made of much stronger stuff.

"Muriel had no right to make promises on our behalf," she said. "So I think we should go back tonight with Brenda and ask her to read the name of the animal in the new enclosure for us."

"Brilliant! I'd forgotten Brenda could read," said Rory, trying to stifle a yawn. "Fish Face, you're a genius. Can I go back to bed now?"

It was agreed that they would catch up on their sleep during the day and meet up after dark.

As midnight approached, Rory and Blue made their way as quietly as they could to Muriel's hutch in the moonlight to fetch Brenda.

The three fairy penguins were having a sleepover, but the laughter was so loud, it was clear that they were all still wide awake.

"I wonder what's so funny?" said Rory, pressing his ear to the door. Unfortunately for him, it hadn't been put on the latch properly and it flew open and he fell through. Brenda and Hatty gave a startled shriek.

"Oh, look what the cat's dragged in," said Muriel as Rory picked himself up off the hutch floor. He looked at the line-up of little birds pointing and laughing at him and reeled back in horror.

"Arghh! What's happened to your faces?"

They were covered in slime and suckers from chin to eyebrows and Muriel had a tentacle dangling off her beak like a turkey's wattle.

"Typical rockhopper. You know nothing about beauty, do you?" she scoffed. "We're having squidskin face packs. Tell him why, Hatty."

Hatty wiped a bit of goo out of her eye with a sticky flipper.

"Because you said, if we didn't, you would punish us horribly."

Muriel tutted loudly. "No, I did not! Brenda, *why* are we having our face packs? Go on, tell Rory."

Brenda shrugged miserably. Some of it

had run into her mouth and, as the squid had gone off, it tasted awful.

"Because you said… *pltheugh*… it would make us almost as beautiful as you," she spat.

"I was exaggerating," said Muriel. "It would take a lot more than a face pack for that to happen. You should try one, Bloop. You have two very large pores on your beak that need cleansing."

Blue went cross-eyed to check.

"Those are my nostrils, Muriel," she sighed.

Muriel peered at them and snorted. "Whatever they are, they're blocked. What are you doing here, anyhoo? You weren't invited to my sleepover."

"We need Brenda," said Blue, leaping back as a glob of squid plopped off Muriel's cheek and almost landed on her foot.

Brenda, who was thrilled at being needed, began to clean herself up.

"Nobody needs Brenda," muttered Muriel. "What has she got that I haven't?"

Blue could think of a whole list of things, but now wasn't the time to mention them.

"Brenda can read," she said. "We need her to come and tell us what it says on the new enclosure."

Brenda was ready and almost out of the door when Muriel barred her way.

"You're not going anywhere, missy!" she said. "I need you to give me a pedicure...

Where do you think you're off to, Hatty?"

"I'm going with Brenda," said Hatty, who didn't fancy clipping Muriel's claws in her absence. "Brenda's my friend and I'm going to look after her."

Muriel pouted, pushed past Hatty and waddled outside. "No, Brenda's *my* friend; *I'm* going to look after her!" she insisted.

"Oh, kippers!" muttered Rory. "Now I've got to look after all three of them."

He led the little gaggle of penguins across the star-lit snow with Blue by his side and, although Eddie and Clive weren't there, it was easier to climb out of the enclosure this time. The fairy penguins might not have been as tall as the rockhoppers, but they were good at balancing, and so light that Rory could easily pull them up. Brenda was the first to go over, but Hatty was a bit nervous and sat on the top, quivering.

"Don't be such a wimp, Hatty," said Muriel. "It's soft snow and you've got plenty of padding down below."

Hatty gave a silent scream, jumped through the air and landed safely in a thick white drift.

"Come on then, Muriel," said Rory. "Your turn to jump."

"I just need to preen my plumage," said Muriel, who hadn't realised the drop was quite so sheer.

"You're not scared, are you?" said Blue. "Do you want to hold flippers?"

"Stop rushing me, Bloop!" snapped Muriel.

"We'll catch you!" said Brenda and Hatty.

Then, with a pitiful cry – "Farewell, cruel world. Tell Warren I love him!" – Muriel threw herself off and landed face down in the snow with her bottom in the air.

"I *meant* to do that," she said, after picking herself up and brushing herself down. "That's how it's supposed to be done. Remember that next time, Hatty and Brenda."

But they had already gone ahead, following Rory down the steep steps over to the brass plaque screwed to the wall of the new enclosure. Thankfully, there was no sign of the dreaded beast so, encouraged by her friends, Brenda stood on tiptoes and squinted at the lettering.

"What does it say?" asked Rory excitedly.

"Um… it says… ooh… I can't read it," groaned Brenda.

"Why not?" said Blue. "Is it a really hard spelling?"

"No," said Brenda. "There's something in my eye."

Muriel got her in a headlock, prised her eyelid open and removed a string of squid mucus with her flipper tip. Brenda blinked furiously and tried to read the sign again.

"Ah!" she said, "I can see now. Whatever animal it is, it begins with the letter P."

"Cauliflower!" said Muriel.

"That begins with a C," said Brenda, "and a cauliflower is a vegetable, not an animal."

"I said *pollyflower*, not *cauliflower*," insisted Muriel. "It's a sort of enormous... flowery... parrot."

"Perhaps it's P for python?" wondered Rory. It seemed an awfully large cave for a python, but maybe it was a giant one.

Brenda shook her head. "No, there's an O after the P."

"Possum?" said Blue. "Potteroo? Polecat?"

They were wild guesses and they were wrong, but suddenly, all was revealed.

"P... O... L... A... R!" exclaimed

Brenda. "It's a polar bear!"

"I knew it!" said Muriel triumphantly. "Didn't I say it was a polar bear all along, Hatty and Brenda?"

But none of the penguins had ever heard of such a thing and nor had she. They were familiar with brown bears, as they lived right next to them, but this polar bear? Was it a real bear or did it just look like a bear, only more ferocious?

"It says here that it comes from the Arctic," added Brenda. "It's the largest bear in the world."

"It's bound to eat lots of penguins then," said Rory. "I don't like the sound of it."

Blue didn't seem to share his anxiety. She waddled off towards the little viewing window, gathered a big pile of snow below it and patted it down hard.

Rory raced after her. "What are you doing? Get down before you make it angry!"

"Yes, Bloop. Get down before you make me angry," added Muriel.

"No!" said Blue defiantly, standing on the snowy step she'd made so she could see through the glass. "If polar bears are the biggest, why is this one so little? It would only come up to Orson's knee."

The little white bear had its paws over its eyes.

"It's awake… and it's whimpering," said Blue.

"Let me see," said Brenda. "Is it a baby?

I *love* baby animals... Awww... Look, Hatty. It's so cute."

"It is *not* cute. It eats *penguins*!" hissed Rory. "No, Muriel, don't bang on the window!"

But it was too late. Muriel had already tapped on the glass with her beak to get its attention.

"Cooeee! What's wrong, you big baby?"

The polar bear stopped crying, took its paws away from its eyes and stared in terror at the strange creatures jumping up and down and waving at it. It backed away, squeaking, ran round in circles, then charged towards the window, growling, in a pathetic attempt to scare them away.

"Run, Blue!" said Rory.

"Oh dear," she said, taking no notice of him, "we've scared the poor thing. Keep still, Brenda. Stop screaming , Muriel!"

Blue hopped down and called gently to the cub through the narrow railings near the cave entrance.

"Don't be frightened; we don't eat bears. We just want to talk to you."

"I don't want to talk to him!" said Rory.

The cub's curiosity finally got the better of him and he crept slowly towards them on his belly. Rory leapt back. He was normally quite brave, but even though this creature was smaller than a brown bear and behind bars, it was much bigger and stronger than he was and it had a row of sharp teeth that he didn't trust.

"Don't be scared, little one," said Blue.

"I'm not scared!" insisted Rory.

Blue rolled her eyes. "I was talking to the *bear*."

The cub looked at them mournfully, then slumped down with its big leathery feet sticking out and sucked its paw.

"I want Mummy," it sobbed.

It was more than Blue could bear. Before Rory could stop her, she sucked her tummy in, squeezed through the railings and waddled over to it.

"What are you doing?" gasped Rory. "Look out! He thinks you're a penguin sandwich."

"He needs a cuddle," said Blue, putting a flipper round the bear. "He's lost his mother."

"He's probably *eaten* her!" wailed Rory. He could hardly watch. He was convinced that any second now, the smallest, biggest bear in the world was about to bite his best friend's head off – but Brenda wasn't.

"Look, Rory! He's nuzzling up to her – he likes Blue."

"Huh! I suppose someone's got to," grumbled Muriel. "Go on, Doctor Bluelittle, don't just sit there wuzzling, find out what it's called."

"What's your name, little cub?" whispered Blue.

The polar bear sighed. "Frosty. I got a sore paw."

He held it up for them to see and, looking very sorry for himself, he told them his story. He'd been born in the wild, he said, and he'd been very happy following his mother while she hunted for seals.

"She hunts seals," interrupted Rory, "not penguins?"

The cub looked at him quizzically. "What is a penguin, please?"

"We are," said Blue helpfully. "Me, Brenda, Hatty and Muriel are fairy penguins and Rory's a rockhopper."

"Oh," said the cub. "We don't have penguins where I come from."

Rory breathed a sigh of relief. "Good," he said. "We don't taste nice anyway. How come you ended up in City Zoo, Frosty?"

The baby bear's big brown eyes filled with tears as he explained. It appeared that he'd wandered off, chasing an arctic hare, and got his foot caught in a trap.

"Ouch," said Blue. "You poor thing."

"Mummy couldn't save me," he said. "She couldn't open the trap. I was there for days." He winced at the memory.

"Sounds awful," said Rory, who had

squeezed through the bars with the others to listen to the tale. "How did you escape?"

"Explorers found me," said Frosty. "I was in terrible pain and starving, so they put me on a plane to City Zoo to be mended by a vet who was world-famous for operating on bears."

"That'll be Mr Bruin," said Blue.

Mr Bruin had worked at City Zoo for years. He was head of Surgery, specialised in large mammals and, when Orson fell out of a tree, it was Mr Bruin who fixed his paw. When Ursie slipped and broke his leg doing one of his silly dance routines, it was Mr Bruin who put it in a plaster cast. Ursie had worried that he'd never dance again – not that he could dance well in the first place – but, thanks to Mr Bruin, his leg was as good as new.

"He was very kind to me," admitted Frosty. "My operation went well, but I'm not allowed home until I'm fit and strong again and it's taking *forever*!" He threw back his head, made a little 'o' shape with his mouth and howled.

"I'm booooored and I'm hooooomesick and I'm loooonely!"

Blue gave him a comforting pat. "Don't worry, Frosty. We'll help you. We'll have you back in the wild in no time – won't we, Rory?"

"*We?*" said Rory.

"You always think of something," said Blue. "You're brilliant at it."

Frosty wrapped his paws round Rory and gave him a massive bear hug. "Thank you, thank you! You will make me the happiest polar bear in the universe."

Rory fixed him with a cheesy grin as his eyes bulged and he struggled to breathe. "Yes, brilliant."

"No pressure there then, Rory," snickered Muriel.

But by the time they got back to the

penguin pool, Rory had already decided what to do.

"Is it something terribly brave?" asked Blue.

"Yes," said Rory. "I'm going to ask Big Paulie for help!"

CHAPTER FIVE

A Funny Tern

R ory got up at dawn after yet another dreadful night's sleep, but it wasn't snowbeast nightmares that kept him awake this time, it was the thought of admitting to Paulie that he had gone over the wall against his wishes. He decided it was better to get it over with earlier rather than later, and went to call for Blue.

"Maybe you should wait," she said, rubbing her eyes. "Paulie isn't exactly an early bird."

"He'll go nuts whatever time of day I tell him," shrugged Rory. "Coming to back me up?"

Blue linked flippers with him. "OK. Chill out; what's the worst he can do?"

Rory didn't like to think about it. Once, when he'd disobeyed Paulie, the boss warned that he would introduce him to his friend, Mr Tiger. It was a thinly disguised threat and one that was never carried out – but there was always a first time.

"Don't be silly. Paulie's beak is worse

than his bite," said Blue. "He would never peck another penguin. He loves us. We're family."

When Rory finally plucked up the courage to knock on the palace door, Paulie was rather muzzy headed.

"Whaddya want? Can't it wait till tomorrow?" he yawned.

"Yes, it can!" said Rory, turning on his heel.

"No, it can't!" blurted Blue, preventing him from leaving. "Paulie, please don't be mad at us, but we went over the wall with Brenda and she read the sign on the new enclosure and the animal inside it is a—"

"Polar bear! Woo hoo!" whooped Rory in a state of nervous excitement.

Before Paulie had a chance to react angrily or otherwise, the noise woke the brown bears.

"Did you hear that, Ursie?" said Orson. "It's a *polar bear*."

"I thought it was a bear all along," said Ursie. "Only a bear could command so much attention."

They seemed to have forgotten all about the abominable snowbeast and, insisting that polar bears were their closest cousins, they wanted to know all about him.

"He's called Frosty," said Blue.

"Excellent name for a bear," said Orson.

"Not as good as Ursie, though," sulked Ursie.

Paulie tried to open his beak to ask a

few very important questions of his own.

"Rory, this polar bear... Is it—"

"As handsome as me?" interrupted Ursie, posing against his tree and flexing his biceps. "Is it as tall? Is it as furry? Is it as—"

"It's a cub," said Blue. "A sad, lonely little cub with a sore paw. It needs our help and we didn't know what to—"

Ursie stuffed both paws in his mouth

and sighed. "Orson, it's a *baby*! How adorable."

"I think we should—" muttered Paulie, only to be interrupted by Ursie yet again.

"Oh, but the poor lickle thing is sad and sore, I can't *bear* it."

Unable to get a word in edgeways, Paulie tried to usher the penguins inside to talk about Frosty in peace and quiet – but that was never going to happen. The bears got very uppity and accused him of being selfish.

"Don't you go into one of your private penguin huddles!" grunted Orson. "You might think you're Mr Big, but that cub needs us. You know nothing about bears."

"I know they're very irritating and

nosy!" shouted Paulie. "Especially the brown variety."

Annoying as it was, Orson was right. The penguins knew nothing about polar bears. If they really wanted to help Frosty, they needed advice. Reluctantly, they waddled back outside and asked the bears' advice about the best way to cheer up a cub that was missing its mother.

"That's easy, isn't it, Orson?" said Ursie. "Bake him a cake."

"Cake?" said Orson, poking him in his pot belly. "That's not for him, it's for you, isn't it?"

"I wouldn't mind a small piece," admitted Ursie. "What did *you* have in mind?"

To everyone's surprise, Orson threw some shapes and broke into song. "Shake, shake, shake, shake your booooooty. Throw him a disco party!"

The penguins stared at each other in disbelief.

"A disco?" said Rory. "Are you sure? Do polar bears have discos in the wild?"

"They have wild parties," insisted Orson, breakdancing round the trunk of his tree.

"Excuse my friend," said Ursie, taking Orson to one side. "You're being irresponsible, Orson. Frosty is too young to go to a disco. Your average bear doesn't go dancing until he is at least five."

"What about karaoke?" said Orson.

By now, it had become perfectly plain to Big Paulie that, although Orson and Ursie knew a lot about how to cheer *brown* bears up, they had no idea what baby polar bears liked any more than the penguins did. It was a problem because, as Blue pointed out, they couldn't leave him like that – not now they'd promised to help.

"A penguin never breaks its promise," agreed Paulie.

"If only we knew what Frosty ate," said Rory. "I thought it was penguins, but when I was in his enclosure, he said that…"

Paulie narrowed his eyes. "You went in his enclosure? Bad penguin! Broke your promise!"

"I went in too," confessed Blue. "It was only Muriel who promised."

Paulie threw his flippers in the air.

"First, the pooping. Then you go over the wall. Now this!" he stamped. "Stop *giggling*, you bears!"

"You said *poop*," tittered Ursie, clutching his sides.

"Ah, grow up and make yourselves useful!" grumbled Paulie. "Try and think of some *sensible* ideas to help Frosty."

Suddenly, there was a loud *squawk* from above, and a strange bird landed on the roof of the palace.

Orson peered at it curiously. "Am I seeing things?" he said. "Is that a new kind of gull or am I having one of my funny turns?"

"I'm an *Arctic* tern, not a funny one," it replied. "Anyone seen a polar bear cub around these parts?"

"Who wants him?" said Paulie. He was suspicious of strangers and wasn't about to give away any information lightly. "What's your name? Where are you from? What's your mission—?"

"Coo-eee... Are you looking for Frosty?" interrupted Ursie. "He's down the steps, to your left."

"Cod give me strength!" screeched Paulie.

The tern lifted its foot, wiped its beak, then hopped down by the frozen penguin pool and sipped some water through a small hole in the ice.

"Cor, I was gasping for that," he said. "I've flown all the way here from the Arctic on my annual migration. I thought I'd overwinter here because I heard penguins were sociable birds. My name's Thermal, by the way."

"Big Paulie," said the boss, shaking him firmly by the flipper. "If you'd care to come this way, you can explain your business over breakfast – a platter of sprats' eyes, perhaps?"

"That would go down nicely, Biggy," said Thermal, following him inside.

Away from the bears, it was much easier to conduct a conversation and, as Rory and Blue settled down in the luxurious hutch, Thermal explained himself. It seemed that he was a good friend of Frosty's mother and, knowing how worried she was about him, he'd offered to combine his visit abroad with a trip to City Zoo to keep an eye on the little cub.

"I do hope he's all right," he said, helping himself to another sprat eye. "I'd hate to go back to his poor old ma with bad news."

Blue and Rory put him in the picture as best they could. Frosty's paw was on the mend, but he was still underweight – mostly because he'd been pining. He needed to build up his strength before the zoo would allow him to go home.

"Mr Bruin doesn't like to rush things," said Blue, "but in the meantime, Frosty is sad and lonely. We want to help him, but we don't know what makes polar bears happy."

The tern stretched his wings. "Lucky I dropped by then, isn't it?" he said. "Got any more of those eyes, Mr Big?"

"I have squid rings," said Paulie, refilling the dish.

The penguins waited patiently as Thermal chewed his way through the snacks, then finally he spoke.

"That's better – I'm stuffed to my gizzard. Now, where was I? Ah, yes, polar bears. What I don't know about them isn't worth knowing. You can't move for polar bears where I come from."

They ate fish, he told them. Lots of fish. They loved it. They loved fishing and swimming and chased after shoals of fish in the sea.

"We love fish too," said Rory.

"And we love swimming," said Blue.

The tern continued. Sometimes, he said,

polar bears would sit by a hole in the ice for days, waiting for a seal to come up for air, and then they would whack it and eat it.

"Good," said Paulie. "I hate seals. A leopard seal ate my best friend, Chubby O'Neil!"

Now Rory had a burning question. "Do polar bears like to slide on the ice?"

The tern nodded enthusiastically. "It's their favourite game, my son! They slide; they toboggan; they ski."

"Me too!" said Rory. "And I snowboard with my friends."

"Good for you. I bet little Frosty would love to have a go at that," said Thermal.

As Blue swallowed another squid ring,

it crossed her mind that, although polar bears and penguins lived poles apart, they had a lot in common – they liked the same food and they were really into winter sports and swimming. "Rory, polar bears are just like us, really, aren't they? Only big and furry."

"Yeah!" agreed Rory. "Knowing what we know now, it'll be easy to come up with ways to amuse Frosty. Let's go and make a list."

"Not so fast!" said Paulie.

Their hearts sank – he was going to tell them off after all. They hung their heads and waited to hear what their punishment would be.

"Furious as I am with you both,"

he began, "I'm very grateful that you brought the suffering of little Frosty to my attention. I would like you to spread the word and come up with some ideas to speed up his recovery by this afternoon. Whaddya say?"

"We promise!" chorused Rory and Blue.

And this time, they meant it.

CHAPTER SIX

'The Windy Song'

Having briefed the other penguins about coming up with ways to help Frosty, Rory was struggling with his own list. Now that he knew what polar bears liked, he was stuck for choice: should he take him rock-hopping, tobogganing or swimming? He couldn't decide, so he went to run it past Blue.

"Tricky one," she said. "Swimming is the best all-round exercise anyone can get."

"I know," said Rory, "but Frosty is used to swimming in the sea. Won't he get bored just doing laps of the pool?"

"Not if we turn it into a race," said Blue.

Rory thought about it. A race would be fun – and fun was just what the little cub needed – but would it be as exciting as rock-hopping? Maybe jumping about would be the best thing to build up his muscles, but would it be good for him so soon after his operation?

"I don't think Mr Bruin would have

let him out of hospital if he couldn't put weight on his foot," said Blue. "But tobogganing might be safer."

"Not the way I do it," said Rory, who liked to think of himself as the ultimate stunt-penguin.

"Frosty's still a baby," said Blue. "He's weak from his injury, so we'll have to build him up slowly. How about doing a bit of all three?"

Rory mulled it over.

"You mean like a triathlon? Penguins versus polar bear. That would give Frosty a great workout. Nice one, Fish Face! I'll go and tell Eddie and Clive. You want to be in the team?"

Blue looked surprised. Usually, Rory

had to bribe his mates with mackerel to let her join in. She was every bit as good at snow sports as they were, but they liked things to be Boys Only, even though they secretly fancied Hatty and Brenda.

"Won't Eddie and Clive mind?" she asked.

Rory held something up in a small bag. "They'll do anything for a squid ring."

He'd saved a few from Paulie's palace, knowing that a situation like this might crop up. His friends wouldn't be able to resist them. There were three each – they'd be like putty in his flippers.

"Come on then," grinned Blue.

They made their way across the enclosure to organise the triathlon, but, as they got near the penguin pool, they were distracted by the sound of music coming from a transistor radio and somebody shouting orders.

"Oh my cod, Hatty! It's six star jumps to the *left*, not the right. Keep up, Brenda!"

Rory and Blue watched in amused silence from behind a rock as Muriel tried her best to put together an aerobic dance routine with her two fairy friends. It wasn't going well, as she was the only one with any sense of direction.

"Three steps forward, three steps back!" shouted Muriel. "Did I ask you to do a knees-bend, Hatty?"

Hatty tugged miserably at the crotch of her leotard. It was the one Waldo had made her for the talent show to do synchronised swimming in, but it had shrunk and was pulling in all the wrong places.

"I've got a wedgie!" she wailed.

"Live with it!" snapped Muriel. "We need to learn this routine fast, so we can teach it to Frosty."

5...6...7...8...

Rory and Blue spluttered with laughter and gave their hiding place away. Muriel snapped the music off and marched over.

"Oh, it's Bloop and Boyf. I might have guessed," she said. "You can take those silly grins off your beaks. Cod knows what ridiculous idea *you've* come up with to help that poor cub, so it's just as well someone knows what they're doing."

"I don't know," muttered Brenda. "Is that way left, Hatty?"

"It's right, Brenda," said Hatty.

Muriel spun round and flapped her flippers at them. "It's wrong!" she screeched. "Get back in line and follow me!

The zoo will be opening soon; we need to crack this before the visitors arrive."

She turned the radio up full blast.

"One-two-three and a leg-kick, and a shimmy and— Hatty, stop fiddling. If you'd come to my Fat Camp in the summer, your leotard wouldn't be so snug!"

Little wonder that the fairy penguins were confused. It was a difficult routine and Muriel kept changing it. As she had her back to them, Brenda and Hatty kept pulling faces, making rude gestures and messing about.

"I don't remember Thermal saying that polar bears could dance," said Rory, lowering his voice so as not to wake Orson and Ursie. "The brown bears like to think they can, but has Frosty got the legs for it?"

Just then, Paulie went past. Hearing the music, he waddled into reverse and watched, agog, as Muriel put the girls through their paces. Having spotted him, Brenda and Hatty were now on their best behaviour, but they still hadn't got to grips with the routine.

"Early days, I guess," said Paulie, trying hard not to laugh as Brenda kicked Muriel up the bottom. "Had any ideas yet, you two?"

"Three," said Blue.

"A triathlon," added Rory. "Swimming, rock-hopping and tobogganing, only like a race."

Big Paulie tugged at his chin and nodded encouragingly.

"I like it! Maybe a bit of healthy competition will bring Frosty out of his shell."

He clicked his flippers and called to Muriel over the beat of the music. "This routine of yours. It's... very ambitious. You may have to dumb it down a little for the cub."

"It'll be hard not to with these two ninnies," puffed Muriel.

Paulie tried to be positive, but seeing the hilarious display of clumsiness in front of him, it wasn't easy. Penguins were graceful in the water, but not on dry land and certainly not if they couldn't tell left from right. How on earth would they be able to teach Frosty?

"Ten out of ten for effort, Muriel," he said. "But try and keep it simple."

She was just going to say something about Brenda and Hatty being simple, when the Arty Party Penguins arrived, pushing a huge block of ice in an old doll's pram.

"There you are, dear boy," said Waldo, shaking Paulie by the flipper. "We've been looking all over for you. Wanted to tell you our idea."

"I'm intrigued. That's a lot of ice," said Paulie.

"Well, it's not to go in my gin and tonic," said Warren, twirling his false moustache.

"We're going to make an ice sculpture of a polar bear," said Wesley, pulling out a nail file and chiselling a chip off the block. "But not just any old polar bear – Frosty's mother!"

"And I have written a poem to be recited in conjunction with the great unveiling," said Waldo.

"He means he's going to read it out when we show Frosty the ice sculpture," explained Wesley.

"That's what I *said*, darling," snapped Waldo, opening his notebook with a flourish. "Will somebody please turn that frightful music off and I'll begin?"

He stood on the rock with all the penguins gathered round him and began:

"It's natural to miss the wild,

Poor lonely cub, poor only child.

Your mother waits and cries for you

And she howls, boo hoo. Boo hoo—"

"Yoo hoo!" interrupted Ursie, who'd been woken by the sound of sobbing penguins.

Orson had also been disturbed. "What's with all the blubbering?" he grunted. "Who died?"

Waldo snapped his notebook shut and waved it angrily at the bears. "You killed my poem!"

"We simply put it out of its misery," said Ursie. "I thought we were meant to be cheering Frosty up. If you read any more of that, there will be tears before bedtime."

"I bet Shakespeare didn't have to put up with bears heckling him while he was reading his sonnets," grumbled Waldo.

The bears didn't have a clue that Shakespeare was the finest poet the world had ever known – and didn't care much either.

"Shall I ignore them and carry on, luvvies?" said Waldo, trying to find his place.

"Boo! Get off!" said Orson. "Polar bears hate poetry. Frosty needs something to make him laugh."

"Like your face?" pouted Waldo.

"Very witty," said Orson. "Probably best if you stick to art and leave the jokes to us."

Ursie grabbed his hat and cane. "What Frosty needs is a tune with rude sounds and actions, like 'The Windy Song'. Hit it, Orson!"

Before anyone could stop them, the brown bears began to sing, hurling themselves about as they did the actions.

"When you're feeling sad and low,
Sit on your bum in a pile of snow!
Wave your legs in the winter air
And break wind like a big brown bear…
Join in, everybody!"

It was such a catchy song, even the uptight chinstraps couldn't resist. If Penguin Cam was recording, everyone on the internet would be laughing out loud to see a bunch of assorted penguins

flinging themselves on to their backsides
and blowing off as loudly as they could.
And it got better; there was another verse.

"When you're feeling lost and sad,
When you miss your mum and dad,
Stick your tail in the air
And break wind like you just don't care!"

When everyone had finally stopped hooting, farting and rolling about, Paulie clapped his flippers for attention.

"That was stupid; that was ridiculous; that was childish!" he bellowed. "That is *exactly* the kind of thing that would make a bear cub laugh – and laughter is the best medicine."

Waldo's beak shrivelled. "It's not what *I'd* call poetry," he said snippily.

The great emperor penguin shrugged. "So? It's funny. I want you all to learn the words and actions and teach them to Frosty. Now, if you'll excuse me, I have to see a man about a dogfish."

Still giggling, Rory and Blue went to find Eddie and Clive.

"I can't wait to teach them 'The Windy Song'," said Rory. "Eddie's wind is seriously loud!"

"So I've heard," laughed Blue. She was in a happy mood now that they had a plan to help Frosty – but would it work?

CHAPTER SEVEN

Ready, Steady...

B y the time the zoo had closed, all the penguins were very familiar with 'The Windy Song', especially Eddie, who performed it louder than anybody, just as Rory said he would. Muriel had added some extra groovy moves into her aerobic dance, Rory and crew had put together a great winter sports triathlon and the Arty Party Penguins had been practising their carving. It was time to escape over the wall and visit Frosty, but how would they lift a large block of ice over the top?

"I'm thinking of winching it up with a rope and tackle," said Waldo.

"I haven't got any rope," said Warren.

"I haven't got any tackle," said Wesley.

Luckily, Rory came up with a good suggestion. "Why don't you cut some ice from Frosty's pool when you get there?"

Waldo thought about it for two seconds and clapped him heartily on the back. "You're a marvel, darling," he said, "I'll fetch my tools."

Under the cover of darkness, the troop of penguins formed another pyramid and, apart from Waldo almost decapitating Warren when he slipped with his saw, they made it over to the other side in one piece. Frosty was delighted to see them.

"You came back!" he beamed. "And you brought friends! Oooh... What shall we play?"

"Play?" said Muriel. "We haven't come to play. You're going to exercise to music to build up those skinny little legs for a start."

"Will it be fun?" asked Frosty.

"Not if you do it properly," continued Muriel, twiddling the radio knob. "You have to go through the pain barrier, otherwise it's all a big fat waste of my time."

Frosty's face fell as Muriel ushered him into the line-up with Hatty and Brenda.

"Copy what I do," she commanded. "Any fool can follow this routine, can't you, Brenda and Hatty?"

As Muriel and the girls went into their star jumps, Frosty tried his best to keep up, but he didn't know left from right either and, as he tried to do a high kick, he accidentally booted Brenda up in the air. She was fine, if a little embarrassed, but he looked as if he was about to cry, so Blue stepped in to help.

"Time out, Muriel," she said, taking the cub to one side. "Don't worry, Frosty, I'll teach you the steps. Once you get into the rhythm, you'll enjoy it."

Frosty pulled a face and pointed at Muriel. "But I'm scared of that penguin!"

"Don't be," said Blue. "She's a bossybeak, but she means well. Give me your paw."

She borrowed a crayon from Waldo and drew a letter R on Frosty's right pad and a letter L on his left, so he knew which way was which.

"Now, it's six steps to the left, then six to the right," she said. "Can you count to six?"

Frosty nodded enthusiastically. "Yes, Mummy taught me: one, two three, five, four, seven, eleventy!"

"Nearly," said Blue. "Just follow me."

They had a practice and, after a while, Frosty found that he was good at dancing. He'd forgotten that he had a sore foot and was bouncing about quite happily. Even Muriel was impressed.

"You're a lot lighter on your feet than Hatty," she puffed as they came to the end of the routine. "Although that's not saying much. Phew! That's enough of that."

To Frosty's disappointment, she turned the music off.

"More dancing!" said Frosty. "*Pleeease*, Bossybeak! Dancing is my favourite."

Muriel glared at Blue. "I wonder where he got that name from, *Ber-loop?*"

"The emu, I expect," said Rory, coming to Blue's rescue.

"What emu?" wondered Eddie. "I didn't know there was an emu, did you, Clive?"

Clive, who was by far the cleverer of the two, decided to change the subject. "Dude," he said to Frosty, "have you ever heard of a triathlon?"

Frosty scratched his ear and looked puzzled.

"Don't worry, nor had I," said Eddie. "Would you like to do three kinds of races in the snow, instead? Swimming, rock-hopping and tobogganing?"

"I love races!" said Frosty. "Best of all, I love swimming, rock-hopping and tobogganing."

"Let's start with swimming," said Rory. "We'll have a little go at everything to warm up, then we'll do the race for real – you against me, Clive, Eddie and Blue."

Eddie looked Blue up and down. "Blue? Blue is a *girl*! Girls can't be in the boys' team, can they, Clive?"

"Rory gave us three squid rings, remember?" said Clive. "You said it was fine."

"It would have been a whole lot finer if he'd given us four," sulked Eddie.

Blue took no notice and made her way over to the side of the pool with Rory. The Arty Party Penguins had already cut a big chunk of ice from the frozen centre, so there was a hole to jump into. Frosty stood up on his back legs and prepared to dive. He hadn't been swimming since his operation – he'd wanted to, but it was no fun on his own, so he hadn't bothered.

"OK, let's start off with six lengths of the pool underwater," said Rory. "Ready, steady..."

Before he could say *go*, Frosty had jumped in. He floundered for a moment and, although Eddie shot past, the others

held back until the baby bear was ready.
Then, they all took a deep breath, sunk
below the surface and swam as fast as they
could, making sure not to overtake Frosty
in case it upset him. His leg-kicks were

a bit weak at first, but by the fifth length,
his muscles remembered what to do, and
by the sixth, he felt confident and strong.
At the end of the race, it was a tie between
him and Eddie.

"Again! Again!" whooped Frosty. "Swimming is my favourite!"

"Soon," said Rory, hopping out of the pool. "We're going to do rock-hopping now."

They all made their way over to the artificial mountain range. Rockhopper penguins were particularly proud of their jumping skills and were known for their great daring, but this was a challenge even for them.

"High, Eddie," said Clive, gazing up at the summit.

"Hi, Clive," said Eddie.

The penguins had a fake cliff in their enclosure, but it wasn't nearly as imposing as this one and it took a lot of nerve to leap between the rocks, which were much further apart than they were used to. The boys stood posing with Rory, full of bravado, but nobody wanted to go first.

"Your turn, Frosty!" said Eddie.

But Frosty was frozen to the spot. He hadn't been rock-hopping since he caught his foot in that trap – could he still do it? Would he slip and fall? He wasn't sure. Blue watched for a while and, realising he needed a bit of encouragement, she sidled over to the ledge he was standing on and jumped off without hesitating. It was a long way down for a penguin and, as she went into freefall, Rory held his breath.

"Easy!" she called as she landed neatly on the boulder below.

Frosty edged himself forward. It wasn't a giant leap for a bear – if a fairy penguin could do it, then so could he. Blue waved up at him and he threw himself off the narrow ledge without another thought. When he landed and realised that his leg didn't hurt, he became more and more adventurous.

After an hour-long session, Frosty didn't want to stop. "Again! Again!" he cried. "Rock-hopping is my favourite!"

The exhausted rockhoppers collapsed in the snow.

"We still have to do tobogganing," said Rory.

"Can't we do it tomorrow?" gasped Clive.

"Can't we do it yesterday?" added Eddie.

Blue grabbed hold of Rory's flipper and pulled him up. "Frosty's waiting."

"Tobogganing is my *favourite!*" insisted Frosty.

He was so enthusiastic, the penguins picked themselves up and joined him on the icy slopes. Having watched him whooshing down on his back, his belly and his head, it was clear that this baby polar bear could teach them a trick or two. When it was time to take part in the triathlon for real, it was anybody's guess who was going to win.

The Arty Party Penguins put down their sculpting tools and came out from behind a rock to watch.

"My money's on the bear," said Waldo. "He has the benefit of size. What do you think, dear?"

Wesley shrugged. "He's big, but he's inexperienced. I think the rockhoppers might have the edge."

Muriel and the girls came over to join them by the edge of the pool. "That bear will beat Rory paws-down," she said.

"It'll be a draw," said Warren.

Muriel laid her head on his shoulder

and agreed with him instantly.

"It'll be a draw," she said. "Didn't I say the tri-alathon would be a draw, Hatty?"

"N— yes!" said Hatty hastily, knowing she'd said no such thing.

"It's tri-*athl*on," said Brenda.

Muriel stroked Warren's false moustache and snickered. "Really? Can you spell 'boyfriend' too, Brenda? No, because you haven't got one."

The race was about to start. Waldo had been given the job of announcing the countdown, but being theatrical, it took a lot longer than it should have done.

"On your marks, darlings. That's it, all shuffle up. Are we set? Marvellous… Did I ever tell you about the time I—"

"Speak faster, Waldo, I'm about to fall in!" wailed Rory, poised on the edge to dive.

Waldo sighed. "Oh, very well… With a one and a two, and a one, two— Hang on, I've got an itch."

There was a loud splash as Rory fell in.

After two false starts, Waldo eventually shouted "GO!" and the race was on.

The penguins and the polar bear paddled furiously up and down the pool to the encouragement of the audience.

"Frosty, Frosty, Frosty! We love you most-y!" sang Brenda and Hatty, dancing about like cheerleaders.

"Faster, you rockhopper chaps!" called Waldo. "Get a wiggle on, Miss Blue!"

It was neck and neck, but, just as it looked as if Rory was going to pip him to the post, Frosty reached out and touched the side with his paw.

"I won!" he laughed. "Woo hoo! Winning is my favourite!"

Whether Rory let him win or not nobody ever knew, but having got the gold for the swimming event, to his great happiness, Frosty went from strength to strength and won the rock-hopping *and* the tobogganing.

"This is the happiest day of my life!" he said joyfully.

"Hooray for Frosty!" shouted the penguins, pleased that they'd done such a good job of cheering him up. But suddenly, his face crumpled. Tears began to squirt from his big brown eyes.

Blue ran to comfort him. "What's wrong, Frosty? Is it your foot? Does it hurt?"

"Noooooo," he howled. "I wanted *Mummy* to see me win!"

"Quick, Waldo," said Rory, "fetch the ice sculpture while we sing him 'The Windy Song'!"

The penguins clustered together in order of height and began:

"When you're feeling sad and low,

Sit on your bum in a pile of snow…"

Frosty's ears pricked up. He peeked through his paws and, as the penguins fell back, waved their legs in the air and did the windy bit, he started to smile.

"Join in!" said Eddie.

Frosty did – and to Eddie's admiration, he was even windier than Eddie. In fact, he was so loud, he started a small avalanche, which made him laugh all the more.

"Your mother would be so proud," said Waldo, revealing the sculpture of the polar bear.

Frosty gasped. "Oh! It's…"

"Yeah, what is it?" muttered Muriel.

Warren looked rather hurt. "Can't you tell?" he said.

"Of course I can," said Muriel hastily. "It's a… masterpiece. Clever you!"

It was true to say that most of the pieces the Arty Party Penguins produced weren't instantly recognisable, but either Frosty knew a lot about modern art or it was wishful thinking.

"It looks a bit like… *Mummy!*" he cried, flinging his arms round it. "I'll soon be fit and strong; I'll soon be home, won't I?"

"You will if we have anything to do with it," said Blue. "Sweet dreams, Frosty. Bedtime now."

"Melts your heart, doesn't it," sniffed Waldo as the little cub cuddled up to the ice bear.

The penguins waited until Frosty fell asleep, then tiptoed back to their hutches to get some rest. If they were going to get him in peak condition, they'd have to keep up his training.

There were going to be a lot of late nights.

CHAPTER EIGHT

The Call of the Wild

Every night for a fortnight, the penguins visited Frosty. By now, he had learnt three aerobic dance routines from Muriel and the fairy penguins and, to Hatty's delight, she was so fit, she'd changed shape.

"What's that round your middle? I've never seen it before," said Muriel.

"It's my waist," said Hatty.

All the dancing had certainly helped Frosty get back into shape. As well as toning him up, it had given him an enormous appetite and he'd put on weight, which was a good thing – he'd been far too thin for a polar bear. Waldo got his tape measure out and, with Wesley holding the other end, they measured his vital statistics.

"My, you've grown!" said Waldo. "You were only this round and this high when we first met and now look at you! It just shows what good food and plenty of exercise can achieve."

"Those things were good for me," said Frosty, "but 'The Windy Song' helped most. I wasn't hungry before because I was sad, but now I'm happy, I eat all my dinner. Soon I'll grow into a big bear like Mummy!"

"How big do polar bears grow in the wild?" asked Blue.

Frosty sucked his paw and thought hard – he wasn't very good at measurements.

"I was only as big as a rat when I was born," he said, "but I'm going to get this high!"

He held his arms above his head to demonstrate, but, being a baby, they were too short.

"A million, billion times taller than that," he said.

"Whoa!" said Eddie. "That's even taller than Paulie, isn't it, Clive?"

Brenda went over to the notice on Frosty's enclosure to find out how tall polar bears really grew.

"They can reach over three metres," she exclaimed, "and weigh more than six hundred kilograms!"

Muriel did a quick sum on her flippers and gasped. "*Six hundred?* That's more than three hundred Hattys!"

"*Four hundred*," insisted Hatty. "I've dropped a dress size."

Frosty wasn't just taller and heavier, he was stronger too and Rory was finding it hard to keep up with him. The cub was swimming a hundred lengths of the pool at night and another hundred in the day when the penguins had gone back home.

"That's nothing," said Frosty. "Mummy swims *much* further than that. Polar bears can swim a hundred and sixty kilometres without stopping."

"Whoa," said Eddie, "that's further than all the way round the zoo!"

"I think a certain cub may be exaggerating slightly, Edward," said Waldo out of the side of his beak.

"No, he isn't," said Brenda. "It says over a hundred and sixty on the sign."

The triathlon training had worked. Frosty could leap from rock to rock with remarkable ease now, and Rory, Blue and the boys had to keep coming up with harder and harder stunts to keep him on his toes. By midnight on Friday, they were shattered.

"Let's have a rest, Frosty," said Rory.

"You've done enough for one night."

"Again! Again!" said Frosty, skidding down a mountain on his bottom. "Not sleepy! Let's do sliding!"

It was impossible to wear him out. In the end, Blue decided enough was enough and thought of a way to make him sit still for five minutes.

"Tell us what it's like to live in the wild, Frosty," she said.

"Oh, yes, do! We'd love to hear all about that, wouldn't we, everybody?" said Waldo, taking the cub by the paw and settling him down next to the ice-bear sculpture. All the penguins gathered round. Apart from Paulie, they'd all hatched in hutches in City Zoo. They had never lived in the Great Outdoors and, although polar bears didn't live in the same place as penguins, they were keen to learn all about it.

"It's wonderful in the wild," said Frosty dreamily. "Where I live, it's nice and freezy. Not like here."

Given that he was sitting in the snow in the middle of a very harsh winter, it seemed a funny thing to say. The penguins were used to the temperature and it seemed plenty cold enough to them.

"How cold is it at the North Pole?" asked Rory.

"It's... brrr!" said Frosty.

Brenda waddled off again to check on Frosty's notice, then squeezed back through the rails. "It says it's minus fifty-five degrees celsius!"

"What's celsius?" asked Eddie.

"It means you need to take a cardy," said Muriel.

Frosty fanned himself with his paw. "It's too warm for me here," he said. "Mummy would hate it in her thick fur coat."

He cuddled up to the ice sculpture and closed his eyes.

"Don't go to sleep yet," said Clive. "I've got a question. What kind of animals live at the North Pole?"

"I bet it's polar bears," said Eddie.

Frosty sat up. "It *is* polar bears," he said. "But also caribou."

The penguins looked at each other and shrugged.

171

"Cari-who?"

"*Bou!*" squealed Frosty.

"Argh!" said Eddie, jumping out of his skin. "Boo to you too!"

"I think a caribou is a deer," said Warren, who had a large collection of leaflets about animals that the visitors had dropped.

"I think *you* are a dear," said Muriel dreamily. "I bet it's ever so romantic in the wild."

"It's very beautiful," said Frosty. "The sky reaches from heaven all the way down to the sea and there are icebergs as big as mountains."

"In the sky?" wondered Eddie. "Clive! Imagine if there were icebergs in the sky at City Zoo. We could do the best stunts, couldn't we?"

"The icebergs are in the sea," said Frosty. "They look like sparkly palaces."

"Like Paulie's palace?" asked Eddie.

"Bigger, I should imagine," said Waldo. "Tell me, Frosty. What else is in the sea?"

"I bet there are mermaids," said Brenda. "I read about mermaids. You lent me that lovely book about them, didn't you, Warren?"

Muriel shot her an angry glance. "He better *not* have done!"

"He... didn't!" fibbed Brenda, suddenly realising her mistake. "Silly me! The erm... the *emu* gave it to me, didn't he, Hats?"

"Yes, for your birthday," nodded Hatty.

"It said 'love from emu' on the inside."

Muriel narrowed her eyes. "I'm going to have words with that emu," she said. "I bet there aren't even such things as mermaids."

Frosty put his head on one side.

"There might be," he said. "There are many strange creatures. There are walruses with great big tusks and moustaches."

"Moustaches, you say?" said Warren, twiddling with the fake one he always wore. "Are they longer than mine?"

"Much longer," said Frosty.

Warren looked a bit put out until Waldo gave him a comforting squeeze.

"I expect it's the climate, dear fellow," he said. "If you lived in the wild, I'm certain you could grow a better moustache than any mermaid, or any walrus, for that matter."

"I've a good mind to book tickets!" said Warren excitedly. "Is anyone else feeling the call of the wild, or is it just me?"

All the penguins' flippers shot up in the air.

"We want to see the mermaids!" shouted

Brenda and Hatty.

"I want to snowboard off an iceberg!" said Rory.

"I want to go and swim with the caripou!" yelled Eddie.

"Cari-*bou*!" bellowed Clive, causing Eddie to leap into the air again.

"Jeepers, do you have to keep making me jump?" he said peevishly.

Even Muriel seemed to think it would be fun. "I bet they have great shops," she said. "Much better than the gift shop at the zoo."

But Waldo wasn't so sure. "I like a wild time as much as anybody, don't I, Wesley?" he said. "But I think the North Pole would be rather extreme. No penguins live there for a very good reason, I expect."

The others weren't convinced and, if Rory was honest, as much as he liked City Zoo, he was an adventurous penguin and he wished he could go with Frosty to see what it was like in the wild. He couldn't stop thinking about it on the way home. His head was so full of icebergs and oceans, he almost bumped into Big Paulie, who was waiting up for the latest report on Frosty.

"Whoa... you almost had me over there, Rory. How is the little guy?" he asked.

"Frosty's doing really well. He'll be going back to the wild in no time, the lucky thing."

The others began to chime in.

"Yeah, I wish we could go with him," said Clive.

"Me too!" said Muriel. "I've always fancied a little place in the country."

Paulie shook his head slowly. "You think the grass is greener on the other side? There is no grass! I lived in the wild, so I should know. You wouldn't survive more than a day."

Rory pushed out his chest. "I would. I'd be fine. I'm cunning and brave."

Paulie nodded solemnly. "You are all those things, Rory, but the wild is not all fun and games. It is tough out there. Fish doesn't arrive in a bucket twice a day. You have to hunt for food and, if you're not careful, you become someone else's dinner.

Plenty of animals prey on penguins. There are no cages in the wild, but there are no safety bars either."

"But it sounds so exciting!" exclaimed Rory.

Paulie put a fatherly flipper round his shoulder. "Rory, when you get to my age, you will learn that sometimes the best adventures happen right here on your own doorstep."

Somewhat deflated, Rory walked Blue back to her hutch.

"Maybe the wild isn't for us," she said, "but we can still have fun."

"How?" he muttered.

She bent down, scooped up some snow and rubbed it in his face. For a moment, he stood there looking stunned, then his beak split into a grin and he picked her up and dumped her in a drift.

"Sure we can, Fish Face!" he laughed. "Let's have a snowball fight with Frosty on Saturday, shall we?"

"Yay!" giggled Blue.

Saturday night came and, as usual, the penguins escaped over the wall and down the icy steps to visit Frosty. But he wasn't swimming in the pool or rock-hopping or tobogganing. He was nowhere to be seen.

"He's probably playing hide-and-seek," said Blue.

"I taught him that," said Eddie proudly. "You'll never find him."

It wasn't easy to spot a white polar bear in the snow, but they tried their best. They split up and looked behind every rock and cranny, but they still couldn't find him.

"I think we ought to call it a day, darlings," said Waldo. "I'm afraid Frosty's gone."

"He's asleep in here!" called Blue, standing on Rory's shoulders as she looked through the small viewing window in his cave. "He's been shut in."

She tapped on the window as the others ran over. "Frosty, wake up! Are you OK?"

The little bear cub swivelled his ears and his head spun round. Seeing his friends waving at him, ran over, pressing his nose against the pane.

"Why aren't you allowed out?" mouthed Blue.

It was hard to hear his reply through the thick barrier of glass, but as he pointed up at the sky and smiled, she guessed.

"You're going home tomorrow?"

Frosty nodded, touched his heart and waved.

"What's he saying?" said Rory.

"Goodbye," said Blue.

Blowing him a kiss, she jumped down and, one by one, the other penguins climbed on Rory's back and said their own goodbyes.

"Have fun chasing the carimou," sniffed Eddie.

"It's *bou!*" blasted Clive, causing Eddie to fall over.

Rory was the last to say farewell.

"Jump an iceberg for me, Frosty. But look out for the traps, OK?"

Frosty put his paw against the window and patted Rory's flipper through the glass.

"Thank you too," said Rory.

The penguins trudged back home with heavy hearts.

"We should be happy," said Rory. "Frosty's going back to the wild where he belongs."

"It's what he wanted," added Waldo. "We should be proud that we helped it to happen."

"Thanks to me," said Muriel. "It was my

idea, wasn't it, Brenda and Hatty?"

But Brenda and Hatty were too upset to care.

"I'll miss him!" sobbed Brenda. "He was our friend!"

"So friendly. So… fluffy!" wept Hatty.

"So get over it!" snapped Muriel, wafting her tears with her flippers. "You've still got me!"

There was no answer to that and when Thermal arrived in the morning, he was greeted by a very sad cluster of penguins.

"Hey, turn those beaks up. This is the best of days! Frosty is going to be with his mother at last. He said he'd never forget you."

"We'll never forget him either," said

Blue. "I wish we could keep in touch."

"No problem," said Thermal. "I'll be back every year and let you know how he's doing."

Just then, an aeroplane went over.

"He'll be on that flight," said Thermal. "See you all!"

As Thermal flew off, the penguins waved at the jumbo jet until it disappeared behind a cloud.

"Bye, Frosty," whispered Blue. "Stay happy... What shall we do now, Rory?"

Rory shrugged. "I dunno. It's going to be boring without him."

But the mood didn't last for long. Just after lunch, the brown bears pitched up with some very exciting news.

"Have you heard?" bellowed Orson. "There's a new animal arriving!"

"Oh no," sighed Eddie, "I hope it's not another abdominal snowbeak."

The rumour travelled fast around the penguin pool. Muriel was particularly annoyed.

"Great! That's all I need – even less attention," she grumbled. "I had my feathers done specially! I thought the visitors would flock back now Frosty's gone, but they'll all want to see the new kid on the block."

However, it was just as well that Muriel had preened herself, because, by feeding time, an enormous crowd had gathered by the penguins.

"I knew they couldn't stay away from me for long," she boasted. "Didn't I say my fans would come back to see me, Hatty and Brenda?"

But they hadn't come back to see Muriel – not this time. They'd come to see the latest arrival. As the visitors waited expectantly, the keeper wheeled in a small crate. As he lifted the lid, Muriel's beak dropped open. Inside was a yellow-eyed penguin – the rarest penguin in the world – and it had come all the way from New Zealand.

It straightened up and looked around, then, friendly as anything, it waddled over to the astonished penguins and shook them warmly by the flippers.

"G'day! My name's Shane... Do you guys fancy a game of cricket? Who wants to bat first?"

Fun, games and a brilliant new playmate! The penguins could hardly wait for closing time.

"I told you that the best adventures often happen right here on your doorstep," beamed Big Paulie as Shane fired up Waldo's barbie and cooked the best meal the penguins had ever tasted.

"Forget the wild," said Rory. "It doesn't get any better than this!"

"Ripper!" said Shane. "Will you teach me the famous 'Windy Song' I've heard so much about, sport?"

Rory didn't need asking twice and, as

the night air filled with barbecue smoke and the sound of prawn-fuelled parps, everyone agreed that City Zoo was the only place to be.